Where does the **water** in your bathtub go **?**

Do **dogs** dream **?**

What do **worms** eat **?**

Why don't **stars** fall out of the sky **?**

Does chocolate **milk** come from brown cows **?**

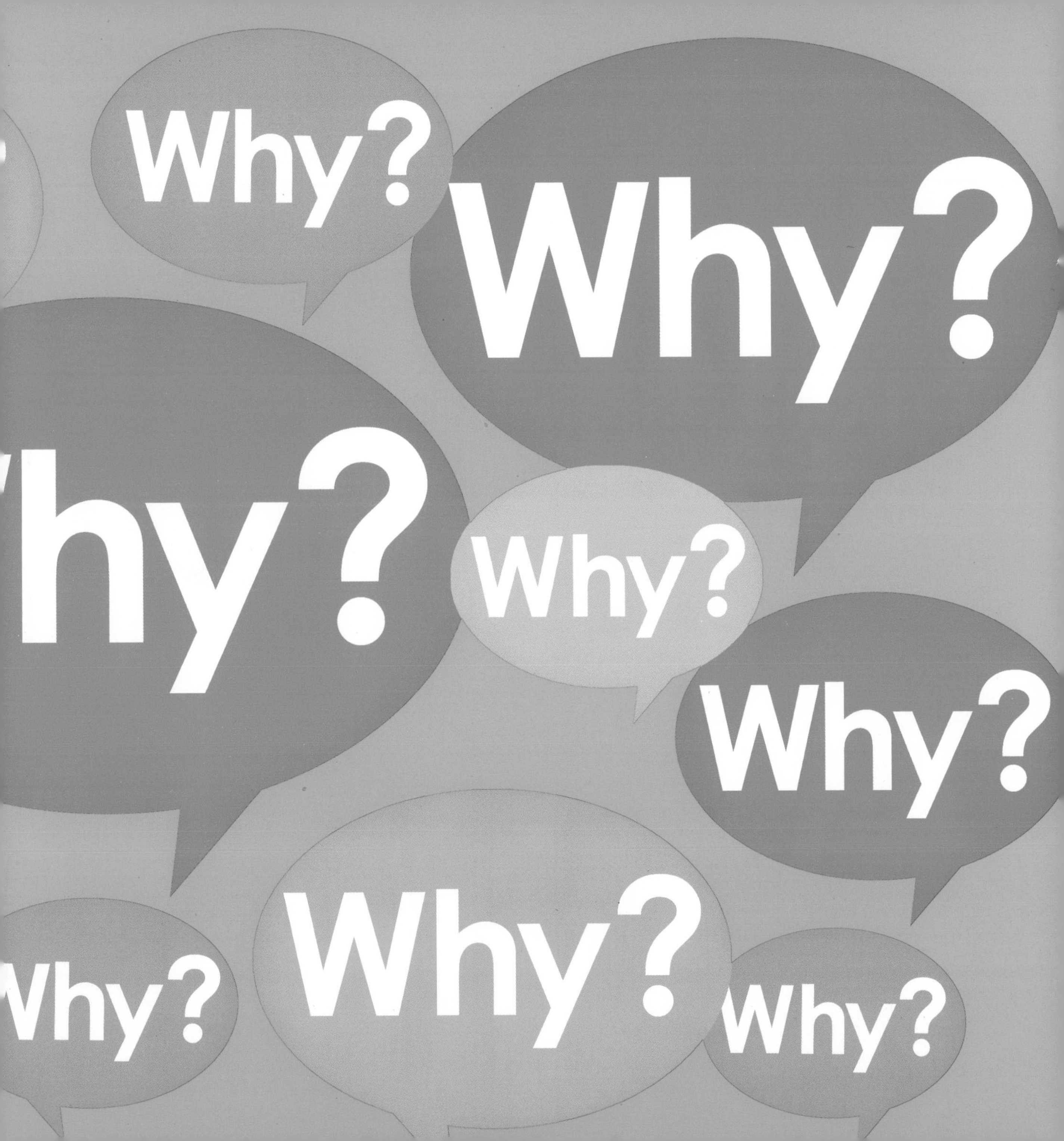
Why?
Why?
hy?
Why?
Why?
Why?
Vhy?
Why?

For my parents, who answered all my questions.

First American Edition 2016
Kane Miller, A Division of EDC Publishing

Text and illustrations copyright © Kathryn Dennis, 2016

All rights reserved, including the rights of reproduction
in whole or in part in any form.

For information contact:
Kane Miller, A Division of EDC Publishing
www.kanemiller.com
www.edcpub.com
www.usbornebooksandmore.com

Library of Congress Control Number: 2015954190

Manufactured by Regent Publishing Services, Hong Kong
Printed March 2016 in ShenZhen, Guangdong, China

1 2 3 4 5 6 7 8 9 10

ISBN: 978-1-61067-460-7

Too many questions!

Kathryn Dennis

Kane Miller
A DIVISION OF EDC PUBLISHING

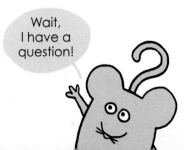

Wait, I have a question!

Mouse was full of questions.

Everywhere he went ...

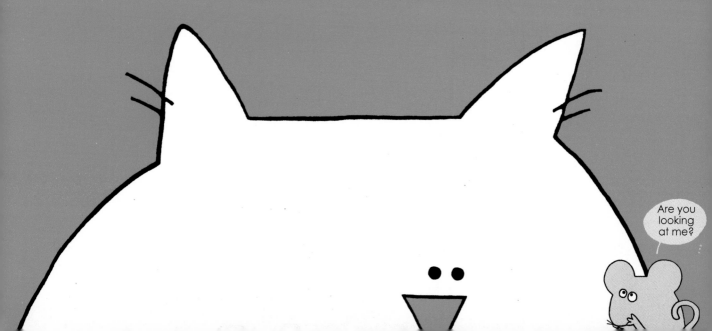

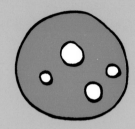

everything he saw ...

Is that cheese?

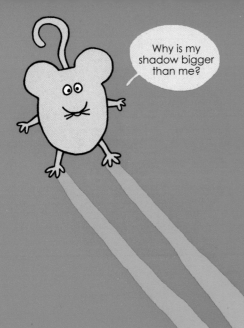

made Mouse wonder ... and ponder ...

... and think of more questions.

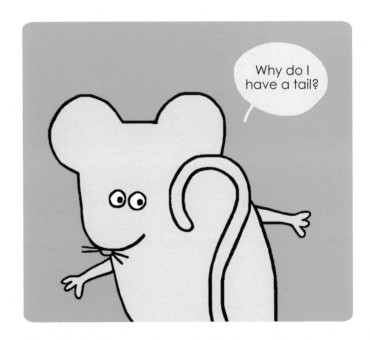

"Too many questions!" his family said.

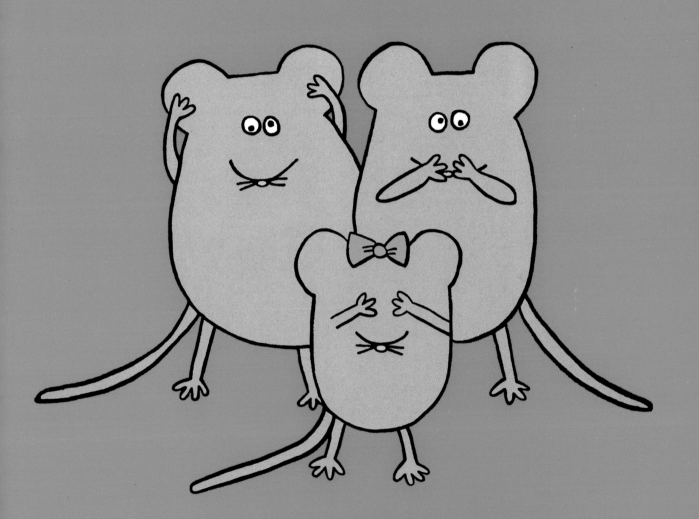

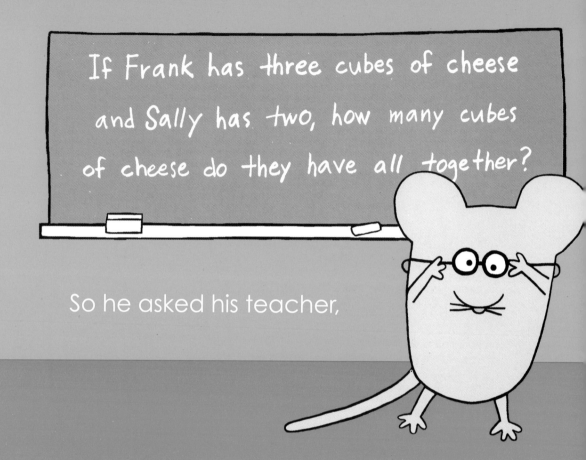

So he asked his teacher,

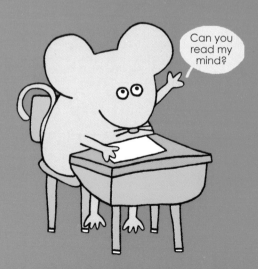

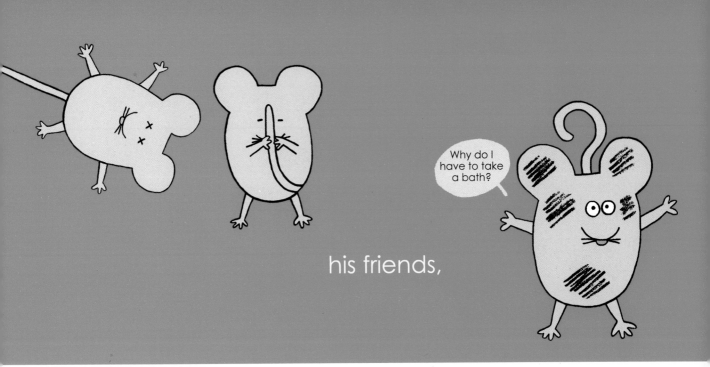

his friends,

and anyone who would listen to him. (Or not.)

But no one seemed to have the answers,
so he set off to find them himself.

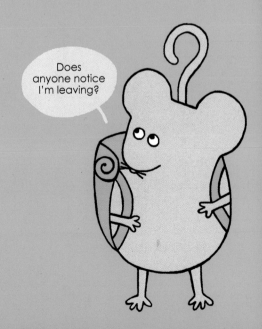

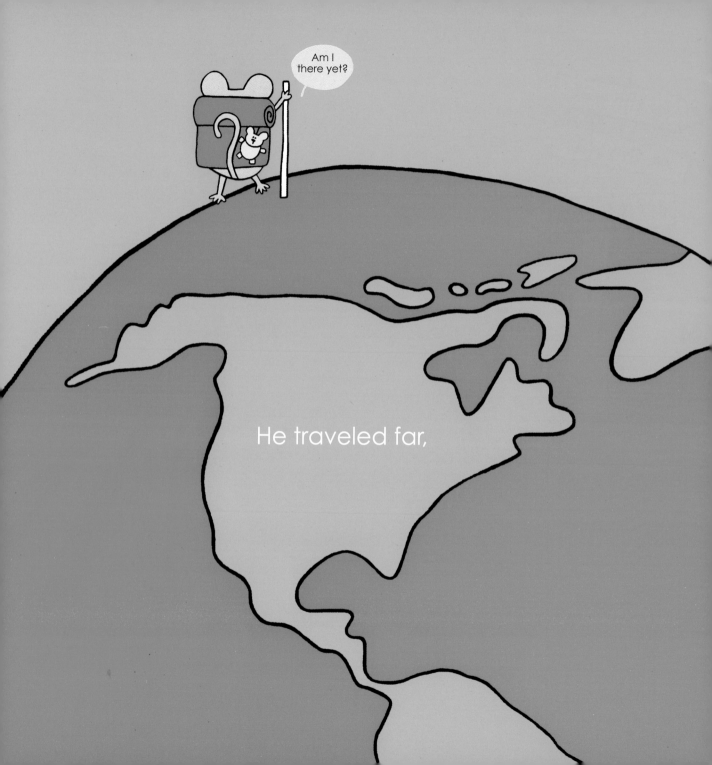

and to the highest high, until he reached a wise man.

"Too many questions!"

"I cannot give you the answers you seek,"
said the wise man.
"I can only teach you how to find them for yourself."

That afternoon, Mouse discovered how
to find the answers.

And more questions.

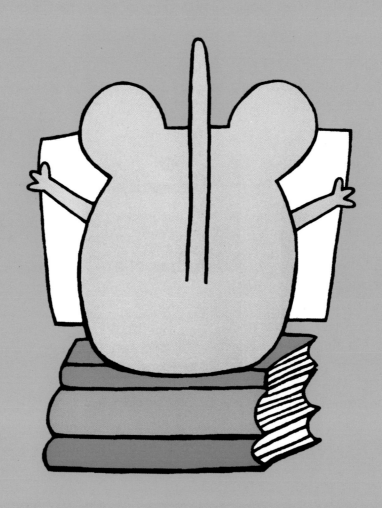

Some of the answers:

(For more answers – and more questions – visit your local library.)

Q. Why do flamingos stand on one leg?
A. There are lots of ideas about this. Some scientists believe they do it to keep warm. Standing in water all day can be chilly, and tucking one leg up close to the body might help. Or maybe they are practicing yoga.

Q. What is snow made of?
A. Snow is made when water freezes and turns into ice crystals. The ice crystals then join together to become snowflakes. When snow falls, it can look like the snowflakes are holding hands.

Q. Could dinosaurs swim?
A. There is no record of swimming dinosaurs, although some may have gone into the water looking for food. Most likely they did the dog paddle.

Q. Are cats related to catfish?
A. No, but both cats and catfish have whiskers. Catfish whiskers are called "barbels." Catfish also make a noise that sounds like purring.

Q. Do pineapples grow on pine trees?
A. No, pineapples are a fruit that grow on a small spiky plant close to the ground, one pineapple at a time. Pineapples look a lot like pinecones, and that is how they got their name.

Q. Can people live on the moon?
A. The lack of air, food and water, makes it very difficult for humans to survive. But who knows, maybe someday we all will be living in space colonies on the moon.

Q. Where does the water in your bathtub go?
A. The water that disappears down your bathtub drain winds its way through pipes to be cleaned, recycled and some of it becomes water for crops.

Q. Do dogs dream?
A. Yes, when a dog makes noises or moves its paws while sleeping, he may be dreaming. Most likely about chasing squirrels.

Q. What do worms eat?
A. Worms eat dirt, which they think is really yummy. Moldy, rotting plants and grass is what makes dirt taste so good to the worms.

Q. Why don't stars fall out of the sky?
A. Stars are so high up in the sky that even Earth's gravity can't pull them down. So when we look up at night, we can wish upon a star.

Q. Does chocolate milk come from brown cows?
A. No, adding cocoa or chocolate syrup to regular cows' milk makes it chocolate. Dairy cows come in many colors: brown, red or black-and-white. But not strawberry.

Q. What makes a rainbow?
A. Clouds and mist are made up of tiny droplets of water. When light hits these droplets in just the right way the light bends and splits up into bands of different colors, making a rainbow. But no one knows how the pot of gold gets there.

Q. Why do baby teeth fall out?
A. Your permanent teeth need room to grow, so the big teeth growing underneath push the baby teeth out. Otherwise the tooth fairy would be out of business.

Q. How do fish breathe underwater?
A. Very carefully. Fish need oxygen just like we do. And believe it or not, water has oxygen just like air. We get oxygen from the air by passing it through our lungs. Fish get oxygen by passing water through their gills, which are tiny slits on the side of their head. They like to blow bubbles underwater too.

Q. Where does the sun go at night?
A. The sun doesn't go anywhere. It is you that is moving, on Earth. At night Earth blocks the sun, shutting out the light. When you watch the sunset, kids on the other side of the world are watching the sunrise.

Q. What are shadows made of?
A. When you block the sun with your body you create a shadow. Sometimes it is short, or squat, or tall, or really big, depending on where the sun is in the sky. But your shadow is always with you.

Q. Where does the sky end?
A. The sky ends where space begins: 600 miles above Earth.
That's a really long, long, way away.

Q. Why do we hiccup?
A. Eating too fast can trap air and irritate a muscle in the middle of your tummy. It closes your throat and you make a funny noise that sounds like hic-cup! Hic-cup! Sometimes holding your breath or having someone try to scare you helps get rid of the hiccups.

Q. Do birds have ears?
A. Birds do have ears, but they are hidden under feathers and hard to see.
So you don't get to see them wiggle their ears.

Q. Why do zebras have stripes?
A. Some scientists believe the black and white stripes help zebras stay cool in the hot African sun, since dark colors heat up faster than light colors. Plus, zebras think stripes look cool.

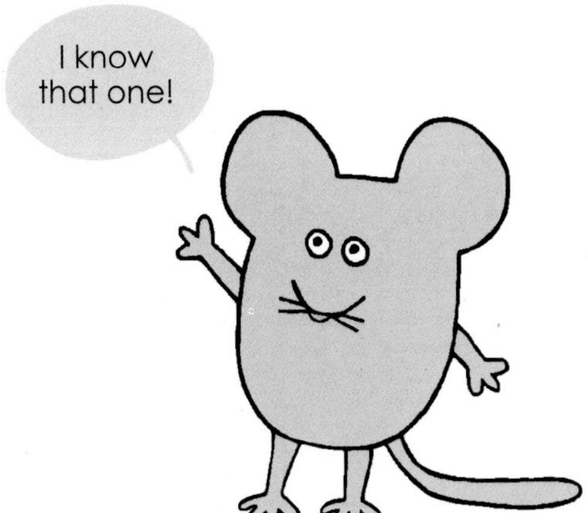
I know
that one!

What **makes** a rainbow **?**

 Why do baby **teeth** fall out **?**

How do fish **breathe** underwater **?**

Where does the **sun** go at night **?**

What are **shadows** made of **?**